Escape from the Minotaur

Written by Frank Pedersen
Illustrated by Dennis Juan Ma

Contents

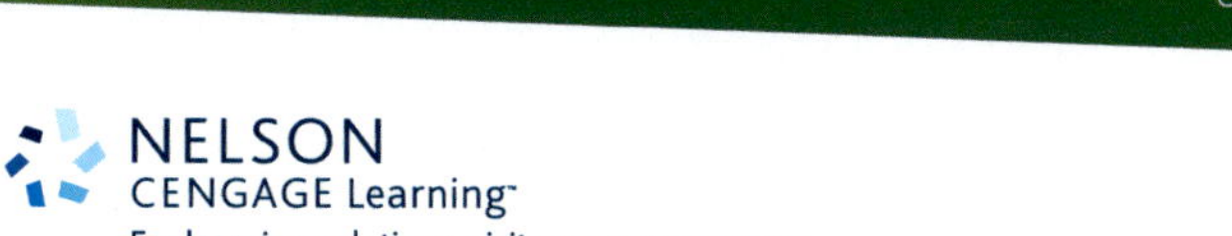
NELSON
CENGAGE Learning™
For learning solutions, visit **cengage.com.au**

Meet the Characters

Exupnos

A young Greek who finds himself in the Minotaur's labyrinth.

The Minotaur

A fearsome mythological beast, half-bull and half-human.

Dear Reader

The legend of the Minotaur, trapped in a labyrinth beneath Knossos Palace, in Crete, is one that has been told for thousands of years. In this version, I wondered what would happen if it turned out the Minotaur was just lonely and bad-mannered, through no fault of its own. I hope you enjoy finding out what happens!

Frank Pedersen

Author

The Minotaur's Labyrinth

1. The entrance to the labyrinth
2. The labyrinth
3. The Minotaur's cavern

1 The Minotaur

"What?" said the Minotaur, munching on a particularly crunchy foot. It spat out a mouthful of toenails and peered at me. Then it let out a loud burp and looked embarrassed. "It's the best part!"

I shook my head. Munching on people's legs as if they were crispy chicken wings was bad enough. But since I'd been thrown into the labyrinth beneath the Palace of Knossos, I'd been horrified to discover that Minotaurs were not only people-eating monsters. They had bad manners, too.

My name is Exupnos. A week ago, there'd been fourteen of us. The advert in the *Daily Athenian* paper had promised a thrilling holiday exploring the amazing maze beneath King Minos's palace here in Crete. The maze was open to the public only once a year. At the time, it had seemed like too good an opportunity to miss.

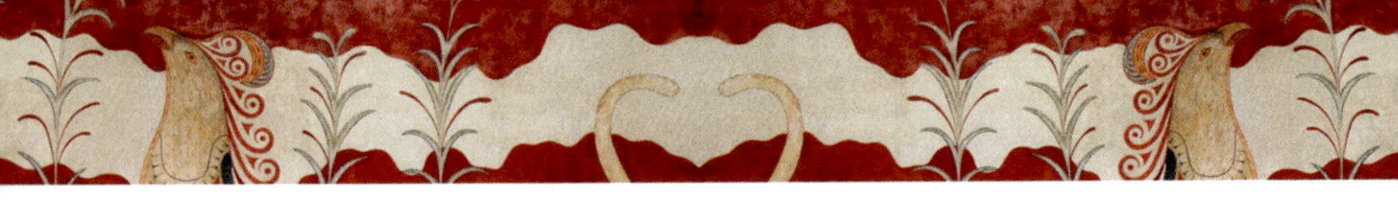

"Tour bookings limited to fourteen places!" I read. "Seven maidens and seven young men."

Exupnos, here's a way to meet some new friends, I thought.

On Monday, I emptied out my savings urn. It was time for a holiday.

At the end of the week, fourteen of us were assembled at Piraeus harbour, a short donkey ride south of downtown Athens. Even though it was a sunny day, the captain of our galley looked up at the sky with a concerned frown.

"Tsk, tsk," he muttered. "Could get rough out there." He gazed at the Mediterranean Sea, stretching out like mirror glass to the horizon. We all looked at each other. No one wanted to start their holiday by being seasick.

"I know!" exclaimed the captain helpfully. "We'll tie you to your seats, so you don't get tossed around by the waves!"

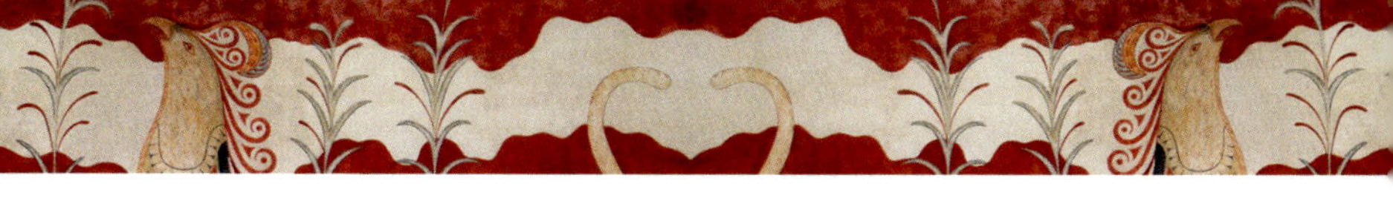

I, for one, was grateful that we had such a good captain. The wellbeing of his passengers was clearly important to him. He made sure that the crew tied us to the seats very thoroughly.

Once the galley attendants had checked that our ropes were securely fastened, we settled back to enjoy our trip. The hatches were firmly shut and the captain cracked a whip. Beneath the decks, we heard the crew dip their oars into the water. Our once-in-a-lifetime Cretan holiday had begun!

As you may have guessed, when we got off at Knossos, we quickly found out that this wasn't just a once-in-a-lifetime holiday. It was a last-in-a-lifetime holiday. Once the crew untied us, we barely had time to rub our wrists and ankles. Then we were herded off the galley and into the palace.

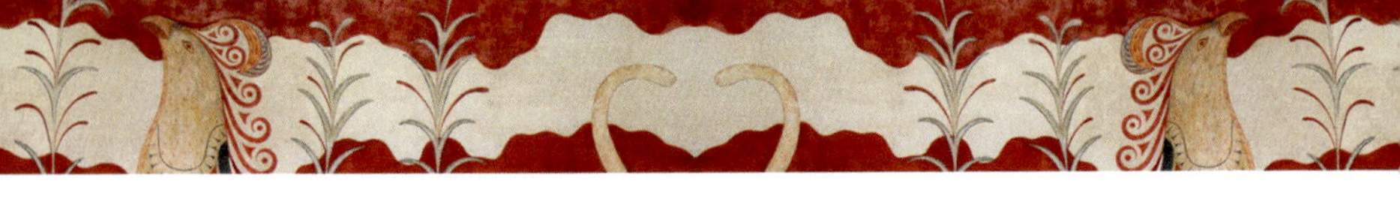

No duty-free, I noticed. That was unusual.

We thought we were about to start our holiday with a tour of the palace. But before any of us could find the souvenir shop to buy postcards, things started to go downhill. Literally.

The tour guides, who seemed unusually well-armed, pushed and prodded us down a long, sloping corridor that took us further and further below ground level. One of my fellow tourists remarked that we were probably going to see the king's underground donkey park, but I wasn't sure about that. I was right.

Finally, after about twenty minutes of descending down the corridor, we came to a heavy cypress door, carved with pictures of a gruesome monster. The creature had the head and upper torso of a fearsome bull. But its lower body was human. Above the door was a sign.

"No Entry to Labyrinth," it said. "Sacrificial Youths and Maidens Only."

I gulped. I didn't remember seeing this in the tour brochures.

2 In the Labyrinth

We were pushed into the labyrinth. The door slammed behind us. There was no going back. Within an hour, we were exhausted. The new sandals we'd all got for our holiday were giving us blisters. We traipsed up and down the twisting and turning tunnels that made up the giant maze.

I'd had enough. I sat down under one of the flickering oil lamps that cast a dim light through the shadowy tunnels.

"I'm hungry," I complained. "And my feet hurt."

My thirteen companions nodded. My tummy rumbled loudly and one of the maidens giggled. She soon stopped. Another growling, thunderous rumble echoed around the tunnel.

"That wasn't me," I said defensively.

At that moment, looming out of the shadows, came a scary figure, its ferocious eyes fixed upon our trembling tour group.

"No," it boomed in a throaty roar. "It was me. And I'm hungry, too."

I've sat through enough boring dinners to know that listening to someone else's travel stories can be pretty dull. So I won't bore you with the gory details. It's enough to say that, if you ever see a tour company advertising thrilling holidays in Minoan labyrinths for tour parties of seven youths and seven maidens, they're probably not telling you the whole truth.

And when they say "meals included", I'd probably ask the tour operator exactly whose meals they're talking about.

Anyway, a few days after the Minotaur introduced itself to us, there was just me left. That's how I came to be sitting in the Minotaur's cavern, watching

it chew on the last morsels of someone's feet and wondering why no one had good manners anymore.

I was trying to be polite and hold my tongue, but when the Minotaur licked its hairy fingers and then wiped them on its grubby loincloth, I couldn't help myself.

"Really!" I muttered out loud.

"What?" repeated the Minotaur. It flicked me a guilty gaze. "I haven't got a hanky. What do you expect me to do?"

As far as gruesome people-eating monsters go, the Minotaur wasn't that bad. It just didn't have any manners. I blamed its upbringing. A monster couldn't help it if its parents didn't teach basic table manners.

Still, after three days without eating anything myself, I was grumpy. I glared at the pile of toenails and bones littering one corner of the cavern.

"You really are a glutton," I said. "You haven't eaten a thing for a year, and then you go and gobble up thirteen people."

The Minotaur raised one bullish eyebrow and peered at me.

"So?" it said.

"So," I sighed in exasperation. "You know you're going to have severe indigestion. Didn't anyone ever tell you to chew your food slowly?"

As if to confirm what I'd just said, a groaning, gurgling sound rumbled up from somewhere in the Minotaur's hairy tummy. The Minotaur rubbed its belly ruefully.

"I won't say 'I told you so'," I said, shaking my head slowly.

"You just did," grumbled the Minotaur unhappily. Another gurgle echoed around the cavern. I looked innocently at a cobweb up in the roof of the cave.

"Oooh," moaned the Minotaur. "I knew I shouldn't have had that last ankle."

I shook my head and continued to look blithely at the cobweb.

"Well," I sniffed matter-of-factly. "Don't expect any sympathy from me."

When you travel to strange and exotic holiday spots, it's not unusual to get a little queasy now and again. Strange food, strange water and strange kitchens can sometimes catch tourists unaware. Most travellers can expect to end up with a mild dose of holiday tummy once in a while. But I was pretty sure that cleaning up a messy pool of Minotaur sick wasn't covered in my travel insurance policies. Later that evening, that's exactly what I found myself doing.

"Eeew," groaned the Minotaur, lying on its back looking forlorn. "Sorry about that."

"It's OK," I replied, looking at the stain that the Minotaur's three-day dinner had left on the floor of the cavern. "I wonder how we're going to get that out," I mused.

The Minotaur burped. "I'm never doing that again," it declared dejectedly. "I've learned my lesson."

"Sure," I said, wondering how many times I'd heard that before. Not from Minotaurs, admittedly, but from plenty of other people whose eyes had been bigger than their bellies.

"Well, let's just see how you feel in the morning," I said. I cleared up the last of the smelly mess and settled myself into the far corner of the cavern.

"Oooh," groaned the Minotaur, burping again.

This, I could already tell, was going to be a long night.

3 Guts and Bones

Hungry. That's how the Minotaur felt the next morning, just as I'd thought.

When I woke up, I found it pacing the cavern, looking at me with a peckish glint in its yellow, bullish eyes.

"Ah," the Minotaur said in a delighted voice, rubbing its hairy hands together. "At last! Breakfast is ready."

I stretched my aching legs and back. That tour company really had been exaggerating when they'd promised this holiday would be five-star. I've had more comfortable sleeps on the rocky Athenian roadside after a long night at the Acropolis temple.

"Now hold on a moment," I said, rubbing the sleep out of my eyes. "Firstly, my name is Exupnos, not 'breakfast'. Secondly, it sounds like we haven't learnt anything from our exploits last night, have we?"

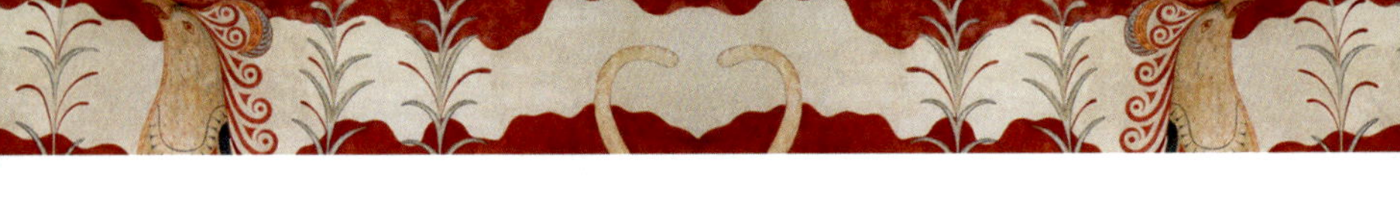

The Minotaur looked downcast.

"I feel fine now," it protested.

"I'm sure you do," I said, looking across the cavern meaningfully. The Minotaur followed my stare and it saw the nasty stain in the middle of the rocky floor.

"I couldn't help it," it whined. "I think one of those maidens was a little off."

"Excuses, excuses," I said, fixing the Minotaur with a firm look. "I think you need to take responsibility for your own actions."

"Do I?" said the Minotaur with a frown.

"Absolutely," I said. "You are a grown Minotaur and you need to make some choices about your lifestyle."

The Minotaur's burly shoulders sagged.

"The first thing you need to think about is your diet ," I said, wagging my finger at the monster. "Nothing for months and months, then you gorge yourself on guts and bones. You know it can't be good for you."

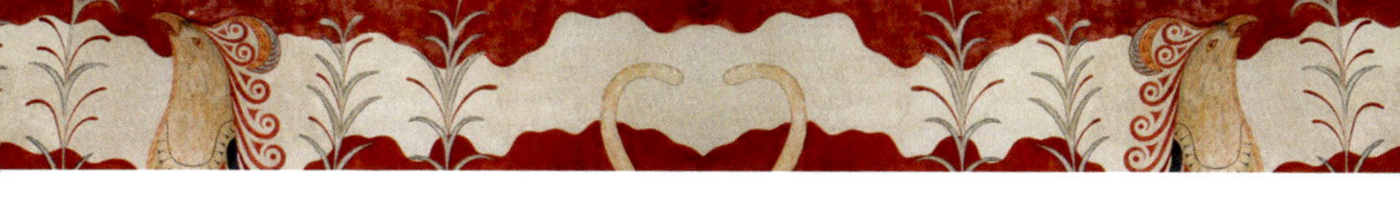

"But I ..." started the Minotaur woefully.

"Ah, ah!" I interrupted, pointing to the stain on the floor.

The Minotaur looked at me glumly.

"There's nothing else to eat," it said plaintively. "That's all I ever get. Maidens and youths. Youths and maidens. Every year, it's always the same."

I nodded sympathetically. I'd once spent a week at my Aunty Xenia's place, where there'd been nothing to eat except cold leftover moussaka the entire time. I hadn't been able to face an eggplant since.

"I bet you'd love a souvlaki, just for a change," I suggested. "Full of lovely lettuce and tomato, dripping with hummus and yoghurt sauce."

A dreamy look came into the Minotaur's eyes and it licked its thick, furry lips.

"Mmm," it replied. "Yes, I would." It lowered its voice to a whisper. "What's a souvlaki?" it murmured. "Lettuce? Tomato? Hummus? Yoghurt?"

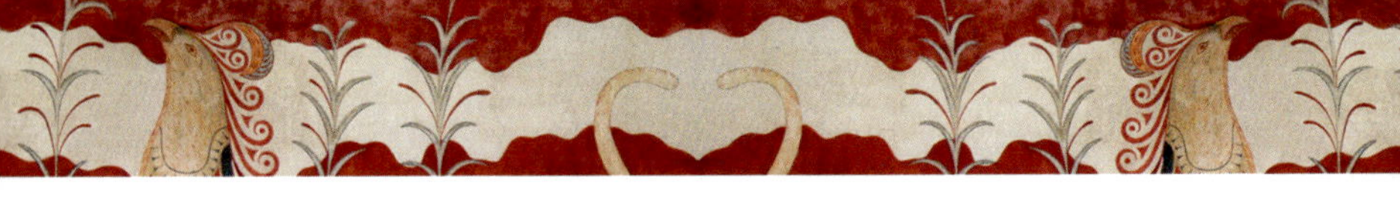

"You've never seen those foods?" I asked in astonishment.

The Minotaur shook its hairy, horned head.

"Then you've probably never tried creamy potatoes mashed up as skordalia!" I said. "Or delicious pastry spanakopita? Or juicy dolmades?"

The Minotaur shook its oversized bull's head despondently.

Even I was starting to feel quite hungry. "You just don't know what you're missing," I sighed.

"No," replied the Minotaur, with a puzzled expression. "I don't."

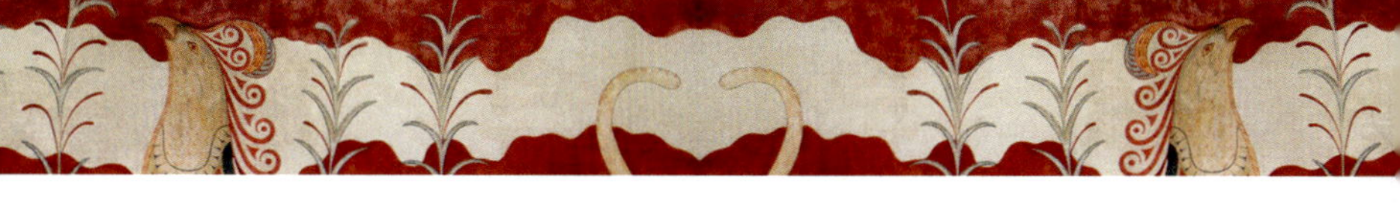

The Minotaur and I sat on the floor of the dark cavern. Our minds were filled with thoughts of our misfortune – and, in the Minotaur's case, imaginary pictures of what it thought souvlakis, skordalia, spanakopita and dolmades might look like.

The Minotaur's belly rumbled.

"But until then, there's always you," it said, a greedy purple tongue playing around its lips.

"Until then, there's me?" I said, frowning at the monster. "What do you mean?"

"You're the only food I see," growled the Minotaur, looking from side to side.

I sighed. This Minotaur really was a slow learner.

"And what happens when I'm gone?" I asked.

The monster looked nonplussed.

"There'll be nothing more for the next eleven months. There'll be no one here to tell you where you can find all those delicious foods. And you'll be all alone in this labyrinth. Is that what you want?"

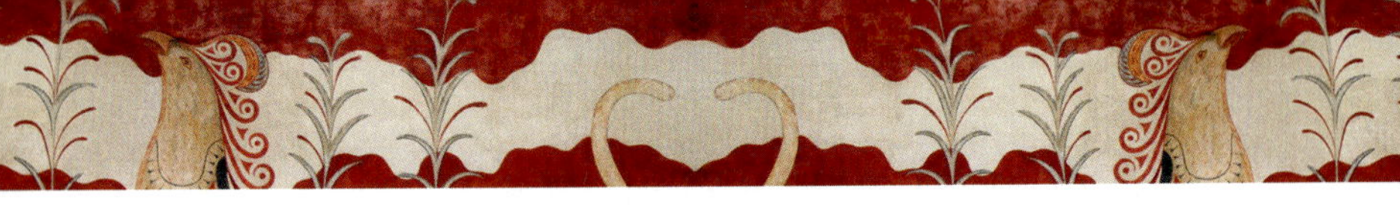

"Well, I ..." started the Minotaur, looking guilty.

"Of course it's not," I said reassuringly. "What you need is someone to help you get out of here. I'm your only hope, if you ever want to taste anything besides squishy guts and crunchy bones."

The Minotaur looked this way and that, lost for words.

"Do you see anyone else here who's going to help?" I asked.

"No," admitted the Minotaur. "But I am still hungry," it wheedled.

"Use your hunger as your motivation to escape," I said wisely, trying to raise the Minotaur's spirits. I stood up.

"Look at me. All bony and scrawny. Wouldn't you prefer a nice Greek salad?" I suggested. "Some ripe tomatoes, crisp red onions, some tasty olives and some sharp fetta cheese?"

The Minotaur thought for a moment, and scratched its head.

"I think I'd prefer a nice Greek," it said sullenly.

I sighed and rolled my eyes. There was just no pleasing *some* monsters.

4 A Clever Plan

After a moment's silence, the temptation of discovering new and delicious foods eventually got the better of the Minotaur. It reluctantly agreed that I was probably more use outside a Minotaur than inside one.

It was a good decision, I thought. I felt comfortable with that particular plan. The alternative didn't appeal, I had to admit.

"Now," I said, thinking about the next step of our plan. We had to work together to find a way out of the labyrinth. "I don't suppose you know the way to the carved door, do you?"

"There's a door?" gasped the Minotaur, looking astonished. "What's a door?"

Obviously that plan wasn't going to work. Time for Plan B.

"Each year, when ... er, dinner appears in the tunnels ... how far do you venture from this cavern?"

"Oh, I know all the tunnels close by here," replied the Minotaur. "Most of the youths and maidens end up within ten minutes stroll." The Minotaur beamed. "It's quite convenient," it said brightly. "It's sort of like home delivery!"

I thought about the journey our own tour group had taken, after we'd been shut in the labyrinth. We'd been lost for an hour – but I was pretty sure we'd retraced our steps at least three times, trying to find our way in the dark maze.

That meant, if we were lucky, the door really wasn't more than twenty minutes from where we'd ended up.

The Minotaur watched me curiously as I wandered over to the mound of gnarled, yellowing toenails that it had spat out over the years.

I gingerly put a handful of toenails in my pocket. Then another. And another.

"They're not really that good," whispered the Minotaur. "They get stuck between your teeth, and they're a real nuisance to get out."

"I'm sure that's so," I grimaced. "But we're not going to use them as snack food. They're going to help us find our way out."

The Minotaur pursed its lips in surprise.

"Come on," I said. "Show us the way to the ... dining room."

The Minotaur jumped up eagerly. We headed out of the Minotaur's cavern and down one of the gloomy tunnels.

After about ten minutes, the Minotaur suddenly stopped. It was dark, and I was following closely, so I accidentally ended up with a mouth full of Minotaur tail.

"Hey!" snorted the Minotaur. "I thought we'd agreed we wouldn't eat each other. Fair's fair!"

“Sorry,” I spluttered, spitting out an evil-tasting clump of bristly hair. “Why have we stopped?”

The Minotaur slowly turned its massive bull’s head from side to side. Its nostrils flared, and it sniffed the air.

“We’re here,” it said.

I peered into the darkness. This was where my fellow tourists and I had found ourselves after wandering the maze for an hour. I looked around. In every direction, tunnels split off from where we were standing.

“Right,” I said. “Head down one of these tunnels. Let’s see where it goes.”

And, as the Minotaur and I made our way along one of the dark tunnels, I drew a handful of old toenails out of my pocket. Every three steps, I dropped one.

THUMP!

The Minotaur yelped in pain.

"What is it?" I hissed urgently.

"E fenk thees ees e deed ennn," groaned the Minotaur nasally. Its hairy hands were rubbing its snout, and its yellow eyes were watering.

"A what?" I said.

"E deed ennn!" repeated the Minotaur in an annoyed voice. "My dose heet dee wall!"

"Oh," I said. "A dead end. Your nose hit the wall."

"Stop repeeding effing I say," said the Minotaur. "Ees nod helpeng."

I shrugged my shoulders and turned around. The Minotaur and I retraced our steps, picking up all the toenails every three paces. Soon, there were no more toenails. We were back where we started.

"Pick another tunnel," I said. The Minotaur grumbled something at me about how come I never

got the dangerous job at the front, and reluctantly headed down a tunnel. This time, it had one arm outstretched, just in case. I followed behind, making sure that a trail of toenails every three paces marked a route back, should we need it.

"Are we there yet?" complained the Minotaur. "How much further?"

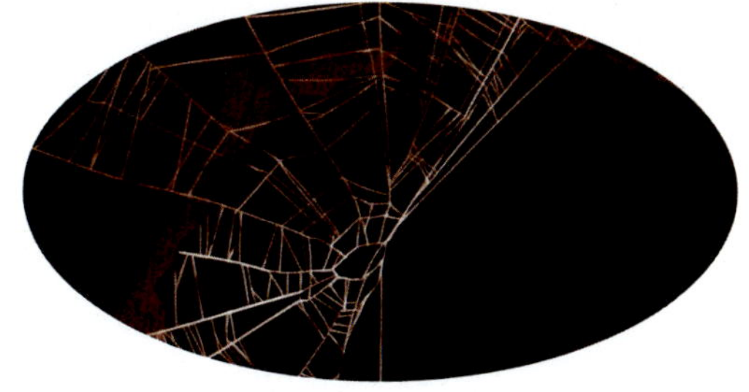

This time, however, we didn't need to retrace our steps. We came to another cavern, from which more tunnels disappeared.

"Excellent!" I declared. "Now, pick the next tunnel," I said, nudging the Minotaur.

And so, hour after hour, tunnel after tunnel, we made our way through the labyrinth. Most times, we came to dead ends and had to rub our snouts and follow our trail of toenails back to start all over again. But, every once in a while, we chose the right tunnel. Minute by minute, accompanied by more than enough grumbling from the Minotaur, and an occasional tummy rumble, we drew nearer to the door.

"Just keep thinking about souvlakis, skordalia, spanakopita and dolmades," I said, trying to encourage the Minotaur.

"Mmm," said the Minotaur, momentarily cheering up. "Souvlakis. Skordalia. Spana ... OUCH!"

I sighed. It looked like we'd hit another "deed ennn".

5 A Legendary Escape

Except, this time, the dead end wasn't a rocky dead end. With a feeling of excitement, I saw that the Minotaur had stumbled, snout first, into a large slab of cypress.

In contrast, the Minotaur looked positively deflated.

"I thought it would be edible," it said, prodding the door with a dejected finger. "Just like all those other things I've never heard of."

"Those things are just beyond," I said. "In a few seconds, we'll be free!"

I scanned the door for a crack or a split in the cypress.

I needn't have bothered. The Minotaur, in front of me, had noticed something I hadn't. It rattled the door knob impatiently.

"Can't eat this either," it remarked glumly.

“Shhh!” I said. I gently grasped the door knob. Slowly, I turned it until I heard the cypress door click free.

I couldn’t believe our luck! I swung open the door, with a grin as wide as our doorway to freedom.

A second later, my grin evaporated. My heart plunged. Glaring back at me with angry eyes was a fearsome Minoan palace soldier.

“HALT!” he bellowed. “No one is allowed to exit the labyrinth. You must spend the rest of your days with the Minotaur!”

“Funny you should say that,” I started. “You see, speaking of Minotaurs ...”

But before I could finish, there was a mighty shove in my back. I spilled out of the doorway. Behind me, filling the entrance to the labyrinth, stood the Minotaur. Its eyes were transfixed by what it saw – not the guard’s suddenly terrified face or the glittering palace beyond – but a deliciously meaty pair of ankles, poking out from beneath the guard’s bronze Minoan tunic.

Before I could utter a word, the Minotaur thundered out of the labyrinth. With a single hairy hand, it grabbed the guard by the neck and hoisted him high above the ground.

"Mmmm. Ankles!" it growled hungrily. Long globs of saliva dripped from the corners of its mouth.

I frowned at the Minotaur and shook my head.

"What?" it replied. "They're the best part!"

"Yes, yes, you've told me that. But, really, think about it."

The Minotaur eyed me suspiciously.

"Have you any idea where those ankles have been?" I said, folding my arms. "A Minotaur could end up feeling very sorry for itself just eating any old ankles out here, you know."

The Minotaur loosened its grip on the guard, and he dropped to the palace floor with a clatter.

"Really?" said the Minotaur.

"I'm afraid so," I said. "It'll be much better if you just stick to normal food."

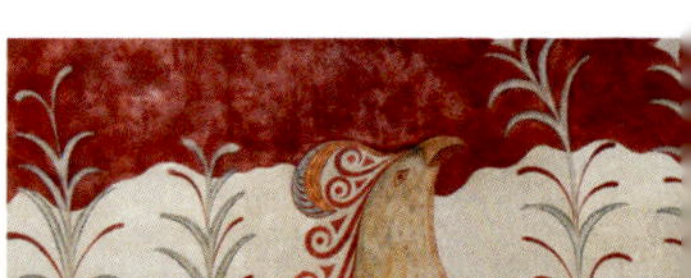

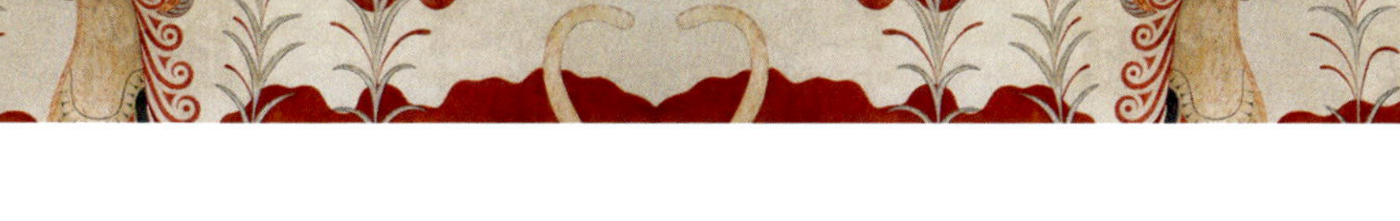

The Minotaur looked sullen.

“Do I have to?” it asked glumly.

“Yes,” I replied. “And I’m not putting up with any arguments, understood?”

“OK,” said the Minotaur, hanging its head and looking forlorn.

I turned around to ask the guard whether or not he could recommend a decent restaurant in Knossos but, to my surprise, he and his ankles were rapidly disappearing down the palace corridor, looking as white as a sheet.

And there you have it. The legend of how Exupnos and the Minotaur escaped from the labyrinth at Knossos. But that’s not the end of the story. Oh, no.

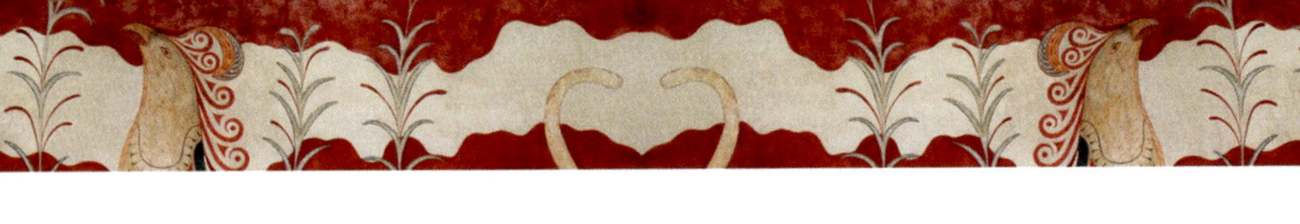

As we found out later that afternoon, it wasn't at all difficult to find a good restaurant in Knossos. Unlike a lot of other tourist destinations, where you're always getting stopped on the streets by hawkers or street vendors or beggars, everyone in Knossos seemed to go out of their way to get out of ours.

We found a nice-looking restaurant and walked in, hoping there'd be a spare table. We needn't have worried. Oddly enough, everyone must have finished their lunches at exactly the same time, because they all rushed for the back door.

It must be a quaint Minoan custom, I thought to myself. Synchronised lunching.

I noticed a waiter cowering behind a table.

"Table for two?" I said, waving my hand.

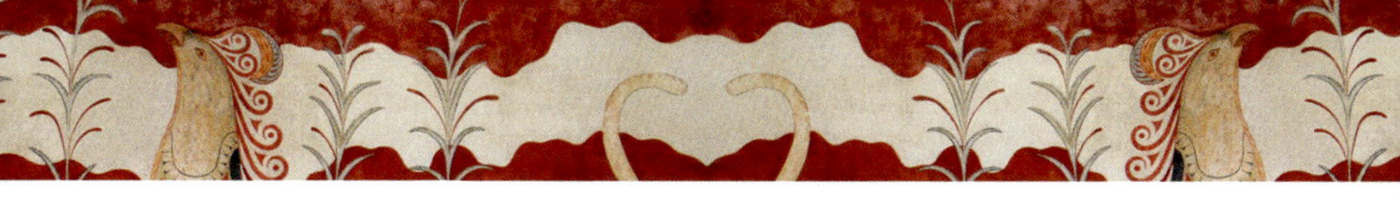

“Our special today is *stifado*,” stammered the waiter nervously.

The Minotaur licked its lips and looked at me hopefully.

“Probably not,” I recommended. Serving a fine cut of beef to a creature that was already half-bull probably wasn’t a great start to its first normal meal ever.

“Souvlakis, skordalia, spanakopita and dolmades!” thundered the Minotaur, who had started chewing on a corner of the menu to see if it was edible.

“Just some olives and a mineral water for me,” I smiled.

The shaking waiter stammered something and edged away from the table. The Minotaur eyed his ankles as he shuffled backwards, and looked at me morosely.

“It’ll be worth it,” I reassured it.

A minute or two later, when the waiter returned to our table laden with platters of souvlakis, skordalia, spanakopita, dolmades, olives and mineral water, the Minotaur couldn't believe its hungry yellow eyes.

"C-c-c-compliments of the chef," stammered the waiter.

The Minotaur breathed in the aroma of the delicious food. It grabbed a gigantic hairy handful, opened its fearsome mouth and ... At that moment, I knew that never again would anyone on Crete have to be worried about showing their ankles in sight of the Minotaur.

6 A Happy Ending

It only took the Minoans a couple of weeks before their dread and horror of the Minotaur decreased.

Slowly, they became less petrified every time we visited one of the excellent restaurants scattered throughout Knossos. I guess they were starting to get used to tourists. Even enormous ones with fearsome yellow eyes and the bulging head and shoulders of a bull.

I'd like to think it was, in part, due to my efforts to teach the beast some manners. There was no more spitting, wiping hands on grubby loincloths or eating fourteen meals at one sitting. And, as we sampled the local cuisine, the Minotaur no longer looked longingly at the parade of Minoan ankles that passed beside our restaurant tables.

To my surprise, I grew quite accustomed to the Minotaur and to Knossos. It was a nice place and, freed from its dark tunnels, boring diet and lonely existence, the Minotaur wasn't such a ferociously terrifying monster. I'd say it mellowed into merely mildly terrifying. And I think the Minoans gradually became accustomed to us, too.

After a few months, I abandoned any thoughts of hitching a ride on a galley back to Athens. I decided to stay. My companion did look relieved when I mentioned this over dinner one evening!

So what happened to me and my fearsomely monstrous friend? Well, like all good myths and legends, there was a happy ending.

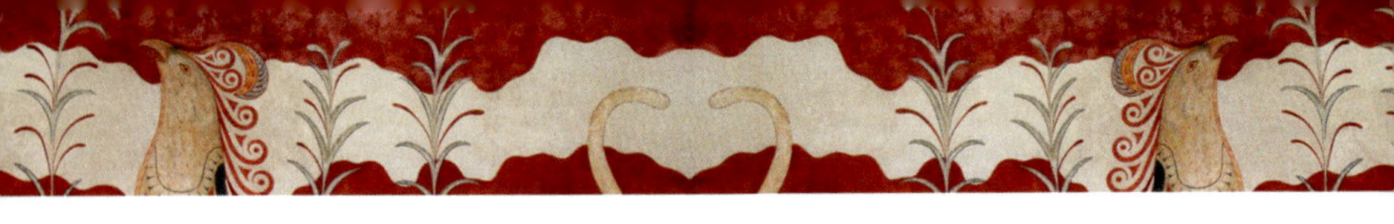

We couldn't be tourists for ever. We had to do something. So we started our own tour company.

Exupnos Gourmet "Taurs". We both thought the name was quite catchy. It's for tourists who are tired of the same old food, day in, day out. We offer them gourmet tours tasting the best foods that Knossos has to offer.

I do the marketing and the planning. The Minotaur negotiates discounts with the local restaurants. It seems to have a knack for negotiating. No one ever refuses. We have a good life, here on Crete. Business is good. People are pleasant. The weather is nice. And we don't have to put up with those awful donkey-jams I used to hate in Athens.

Hey, maybe you'd like to come and join us on one of our tours! We'd love to see you.

But, as I mentioned earlier, it'd probably pay to look closely at the menus we offer. There, in the small print at the bottom of our brochures, it says "all meals included".

And you know I *did* warn you about that.

Despite the best intentions, even a well-behaved Minotaur gets a hankering for good old-fashioned comfort food now and again.

You can't blame it, really. You should see the ankles on some of the tourists these days!